JAMESTOWN

# THE
# CONTEMPORARY
# READER

VOLUME 3, NUMBER 5

Mc
Graw
Hill **Glencoe
McGraw-Hill**

New York, New York    Columbus, Ohio    Chicago, Illinois    Peoria, Illinois    Woodland Hills, California

JAMESTOWN EDUCATION

*Glencoe/McGraw-Hill*

A Division of The **McGraw·Hill** Companies

Send all inquiries to:
Glencoe/McGraw-Hill
8787 Orion Place
Columbus, OH 43240-4027

ISBN: 0-07-827364-1

Printed in the United States of America

1 2 3 4 5 6 7 8 9 10  113  08 07 06 05 04 03 02

# CONTENTS

**1 EARLY AMERICAN HIGH-RISES**
*What makes a visit to this national park a unique experience?*

**8 TAKE A HIKE**
*What do America's scenic hiking trails offer to nature lovers?*

**18 CURIOUS COLLECTIONS**
*Are there museums for everything?*

**26 HURRICANE!**
*Why do people on the coasts fear hurricanes?*

**36 THE SHAKERS: LIVING THE SIMPLE LIFE**
*Who made the simple, beautiful Shaker furniture that is so popular today?*

**46** TEEN TITANS OF BUSINESS
*How did three teenagers make their marks on the business world?*

**56** STRANGE STORIES OF THE SEA
*When is a fish tale more than a myth?*

**64** LEARNING ABOUT YOU
*How can you learn more about that fascinating topic—yourself?*

**72** KALEIDOSCOPES
*How can two mirrors, a cardboard tube, and some tape make the world beautiful?*

**80** THE FIRST FIRST LADIES
*How did the wives of the early U.S. presidents act in their roles as First Ladies?*

# Pronunciation Key

| | | | |
|---|---|---|---|
| ă | mat | o͞o | food |
| ā | date | o͝o | look |
| â | bare | ŭ | drum |
| ä | father | yo͞o | cute |
| ĕ | wet | û | fur |
| ē | see | *th* | **th**en |
| ĭ | tip | th | **th**in |
| ī | ice | hw | **wh**ich |
| î | pierce | zh | u**s**ual |
| ŏ | hot | ə | **a**lone |
| ō | no | | op**e**n |
| ô | law | | pen**c**il |
| oi | boil | | lem**o**n |
| ou | loud | | camp**u**s |

# ❖ EARLY AMERICAN ❖
# HIGH-RISES

*What makes a visit to this national park a unique experience?*

1 Every year thousands of tourists flock to a remote area in southwest Colorado. They travel 21 miles up a winding mountain road to a place 7,000 feet above sea level. What draws them to this difficult location? They come to explore the spectacular cliff dwellings built by an ancient people about 800 years ago. And Mesa Verde [mā´ sä vĕr´ dā] does not disappoint them.

## The Cliff Dwellings

2 Mesa Verde got its name from Spanish explorers who came near the site but did not investigate it. The flat-topped high country covered with evergreen trees reminded them of a "green

**The first high-rise buildings in America were multistory cliff dwellings built by an ancient people, the Anasazi. Here is the largest of these buildings, now called Cliff Palace.**

table"—in Spanish, *mesa verde*. Like tables, the mesas within the park have flat tops and very steep sides. Dwellings were built in the natural caves on the sides of these rugged cliffs.

3     There are about 600 cliff dwellings at Mesa Verde. Most of them have five rooms or fewer. Some, however, are more like high-rise apartment buildings, with two, three, or four stories. These larger buildings contain many rooms built next to and on top of one another. Each room is small and has a narrow doorway. Ladders or stone steps were built to allow people to move from one floor to another.

4     The walls of the buildings are constructed of large sandstone blocks. Between the blocks is mortar[1] made by mixing dirt and ashes with water. The mortar helps keep the sandstone in place. Many small stones wedged between the blocks help strengthen the walls.

5     Some of the truly magnificent dwellings are open to visitors. The largest of the cliff dwellings is Cliff Palace, which has nearly 200 rooms. Some sections of the dwelling are four stories high. Around the building are 23 kivas [kē´väz], special underground rooms used for ceremonies. To view Cliff Palace, visitors must first hike about 100 feet down a steep, uneven trail. Once in the

---

[1] mortar: a concrete-like mixture that hardens as it dries; it is used to hold stones or bricks together

**Spruce Tree House is one of the most often visited cliff dwellings in Mesa Verde National Park in Colorado.**

dwelling, they must climb up four ladders to see the rooms at various levels.

6      Another popular site is Long House, the second-largest cliff dwelling. To get there, visitors first drive along a winding road for 12 miles. Then they must walk up and down steep trails for another mile.

7      Spruce Tree House is the third-largest cliff dwelling. There is just one steep trail down to the entrance. Since there are no steps or ladders to climb within the house, many people come to view its 140 rooms and 9 kivas.

8      For those people who enjoy a real challenge, Balcony House is the place to visit. It has only 40 rooms to see, but getting there requires major muscle power. First there is a hike of 100 feet down a steep trail. Next comes a climb up a ladder 32 feet high. Then it's time to wiggle

through a tunnel 12 feet long. Once inside
Balcony House, visitors must climb another
60 feet of ladders and steps.

### The Ancient Builders

9  Little is known about the people who built their
homes on the sides of these cliffs. Archaeologists
and others who have studied the artifacts[2] found
on the site think that the first inhabitants came to
the area in about A.D. 600. For hundreds of years
they lived and farmed on the top of the mesa.
Then, in about the year A.D. 1150, the people
began to leave the mesa top and move into
homes in the cliffs.

10  No one knows why the people did this. The
cliff houses offered some protection from hot
weather, but the rooms were damp and dark
compared with the older homes on the mesa top.
It was much harder to move around too. People
had to use ladders or stone steps to get from
room to room. In addition, the inhabitants still
had to climb to the top of the mesa every day to
tend to their crops.

11  Another puzzling question is why the people
abandoned their homes. About 100 years after
the cliff dwellings were built, everybody left the
area and never returned. Some scientists think a

---

[2] artifact: any object made by humans

drought[3] forced the people to leave. Little or no rain fell for 23 years. The few springs of water in the area dried up. In addition, hundreds of years of farming had used up the minerals in the soil. The ancient cliff dwellers probably moved to other places where the water supply and the soil were better. Over time the people forgot about their homes on Mesa Verde.

### Rediscovering Mesa Verde

12  For more than 500 years, the cliff dwellings at Mesa Verde slowly fell into ruin. Walls crumbled in the rain and snow. Wooden beams rotted in the sun. Snakes and lizards slithered through the rooms. Hawks and eagles took over the site.

13  Finally, in the 1870s, a few people began to learn about the magnificent ruins of Mesa Verde. Prospectors[4] and miners searching the area for gold and

**This Anasazi jar was found near Mesa Verde.**

---

[3] drought: a long period of dry weather
[4] prospector: a person who searches for valuable ores or minerals

silver stumbled upon the site. Some of them told others what they had seen.

14    More people became aware of the cliff dwellings in the late 1800s. Two ranchers were looking for lost cattle when they spotted the largest of the cliff dwellings and named it "Cliff Palace." Their relatives spent the next four years exploring the area and collecting many items from the dwellings. Others soon arrived and did the same.

15    A few people were afraid that the cliff dwellings would be destroyed. They began seeking a way to save the site. Bills were introduced in Congress to make Mesa Verde a national park. Finally, on June 29, 1906, President Theodore Roosevelt signed such a bill. Once Mesa Verde became a park, it was protected by a law that makes it a crime to take items from national parks. Repair work began on some of the known sites. Artifacts were saved, new excavations[5] were started, and other improvements were made.

16    Mesa Verde is a unique place. Among all U.S. national parks, it is the only one that was established to preserve the work of prehistoric[6] people. Visitors to the site can get a feel for how

---

[5] excavation: an area uncovered by digging
[6] prehistoric: existing before written history

the ancient cliff dwellers lived, and they can stand in awe of these people's accomplishments. ◆

**MESA VERDE: A TIME LINE**

about 600 ..................Ancient people settle on top of Mesa Verde.

about 1150 ................The people begin to move into large, multi-room houses built into the sides of the cliffs.

about 1300 ................The people leave Mesa Verde.

about 1870 ................The cliff houses are rediscovered.

1906 ...........................Mesa Verde becomes a national park.

---

**QUESTIONS**

1. How were the cliff dwellings made?
2. Which of the four houses mentioned would you like to visit? Why?
3. Why was it difficult to live in the cliff houses?
4. What do scientists think caused the cliff dwellers to leave the area?
5. How did people learn about the ruins at Mesa Verde?
6. How did making Mesa Verde a national park help to preserve the cliff dwellings?

# TAKE A HIKE

*What do America's scenic hiking trails offer to nature lovers?*

1   Do you ever feel the urge to escape life in the city and soak up some of nature's beauty? Do you want to prove you have the right stuff? Do you have about six months to spare? If so, you're in luck. The United States has dozens of long-distance hiking trails for you to try. Maybe you'd like to consider hiking one of the three most scenic long-distance trails in America.

## Appalachian National Scenic Trail

2   The oldest and perhaps best-known long-distance trail in the United States is the Appalachian [ăp´ə lā´chən *or* ăp´ə lăch´ən] National Scenic Trail (AT). Running along the crests and ridges of the Appalachian Mountain range, the trail extends for 2,144 miles through 13 states.

**On a beautiful day, almost everyone enjoys a short hike in the great outdoors. But for a real challenge, why not try one of the national long-distance hiking trails?**

3      The AT is near the large cities of the East
Coast and attracts thousands of visitors each year.
Many people enjoy hiking parts of the trail for a
day or a weekend. While these day-hikers can
have a great time on the trail, the through-hikers
are probably the ones who get the most out of
their experience. Through-hikers walk the trail
from end to end. With luck, they can do this in a
single year. Most begin in Georgia in late March
or early April. Then, one foot after the other, they
walk more than 2,000 miles to Mount Katahdin
[kə tä´dən] in Maine by October 15, just before
the first snows of winter begin.

4      How many people through-hike the AT each
year? It used to be almost unheard of to finish the
trail in one year, but then the number of through-
hikers began to grow. In 1998 alone, about 300
"end-to-enders" accepted the challenge and
completed the trip.  All kinds of people have
through-hiked, including a blind hiker with a guide
dog and a 67-year-old grandmother who hiked in
sneakers and carried her equipment in a duffel bag.[1]

5      The trail itself varies greatly. It can be a wide,
soft path through the pine trees or a rock-strewn
single track over a steep mountain. Hikers must
pay attention to the white rectangular trail
signs—called blazes—on trees, rocks, and poles

---

[1] duffel bag: a large cloth bag used to carry personal
belongings

**Three of the most popular trails in the United States are the Appalachian, Pacific Crest, and Continental Divide trails. Each trail has a unique character.**

to make sure they don't get lost. The AT provides shelters along the trail for tired hikers to sleep in. But there are no restaurants or motels along the way. If hikers want to spend the night in a warm, dry bed, they must walk off the trail, usually at least a few miles, into the nearest town.

### Pacific Crest National Scenic Trail

6   The 2,650-mile Pacific Crest National Scenic Trail challenges hikers with a variety of both harsh and beautiful natural regions. It begins in a high desert area at the border between Mexico and

**Mount Hood in the Cascade Mountain Range is one of the sights enjoyed by hikers along the Pacific Crest National Scenic Trail.**

California. Then it travels over the rugged[2] Sierra Nevada [sē ĕr´ə nə văd´ə] mountains in California and into the Cascade Range in Oregon and Washington. It ends at the Canadian border. The highest point on the trail is a lofty 13,200 feet— more than two miles above sea level.

7    To hike this trail, you have to be tough. You must sleep outside every night, regardless of the weather, because there are no shelters along the

_____

[2] rugged: having a rough, uneven surface

way. The climbs and the descents are steeper than those on the Appalachian Trail. Since the trail is so rough, not many people complete it in a single year. Although a few hikers have walked the entire trail in about six months, most hike only short stretches at a time. That means they walk a different part of the trail every summer for several years until they have hiked the entire trail.

## Continental Divide National Scenic Trail

8 Perhaps the most rugged long-distance trail in the United States is the Continental Divide National Scenic Trail (CDT). This trail runs along the backbone of the continent—the Rocky Mountains. It passes through five states on its way from Mexico to Canada, New Mexico, Colorado, Wyoming, Idaho, and Montana. Many of the trail's 3,260 miles travel through some of the most remote[3] places in the United States.

9    Hiking the CDT takes preparation. Since there are very few towns along the way, hikers must carry in their backpacks everything needed for survival. Bears are a constant danger at various points on the trail. Getting lost is a real possibility because the trail is not yet finished— not all of it is marked with signposts or blazes on trees. Hikers must take detailed maps and compasses on their trips. Understandably, only

-------

[3] remote: located far away from cities; isolated

**Camping and hiking equipment are necessary for comfort and safety on the trail.**

about a dozen hikers try to walk the entire trail in a season. Fewer than that number actually complete the route during one season.

### Preparing for a Long-Distance Hike

10 Some people spend as much time getting ready for a long-distance hike as they do actually walking. That's because good planning is absolutely essential.[4] Here are the bare necessities of life on the trail, in case you want to take a long hike someday.

11 • Shoes and socks: Buy the best, most comfortable hiking shoe you can afford. Shoes that fit poorly or fall apart under tough conditions will certainly ruin your trip. Also,

---

[4] essential: necessary

wear a combination of sock liners and wool socks. Stay away from cotton socks because they hold moisture, and no one likes wet feet.

12 • Backpack: Your backpack is your home away from home while you are hiking. Pick a backpack that feels comfortable to you when it is fully loaded. Nothing beats trying the pack on yourself. What feels good to someone else may not feel right on you.

13 • Water: Drinking unsafe water from ponds and lakes along the trail can cause stomach problems. Dissolving iodine[5] [ī′ ə dīn′] tablets in water is one way to purify it. Another way to make sure that water is safe is to boil it for at least 10 minutes.

14 • Food: Most hikers find that one-pot meals are quick, easy, and tasty. Pack light containers of noodles, cheese, canned meats, dried beans, and soup mixes to make these meals.

**This long-distance hiker on the Continental Divide Trail carries a well-stocked backpack.**

---

[5] iodine: an antiseptic that kills germs and bacteria

15   • Tent and sleeping bag: One important rule is the lighter, the better. Choose a light tent that is easy to set up and big enough to hold you and your equipment. Pick a sleeping bag that will keep you warm in the temperatures you expect to encounter.[6]

**Trail Tips**

16   To have a safe and memorable hiking trip, keep the following tips in mind.

17   • No trail is 100 percent safe. In addition to the natural dangers, there are dangers from other humans. Stay away from people who make you feel uncomfortable.

18   • Take nothing but photographs and leave nothing but footprints. Good hikers change the trail as little as possible. They stay on the trail itself, they don't leave litter behind, and they never pick wildflowers or uproot plants. On some trails, such as the CDT, hikers protect fragile plants by jumping over them from rock to rock.

19   • Don't overdo it on the first few days; instead, take it easy as you begin your journey. Most muscle injuries happen because your body isn't tough enough for the trail yet.

---

[6] encounter: to face; to experience

### The Thrill of Victory, The Agony of the Feet

20  Why do people put themselves through the hardships of long-distance hiking? Some do it to get back to nature and to get a break from the hectic pace of urban life. Others do it to test themselves physically and mentally—to find out whether they can survive in a world without the comforts most of us take for granted. Through-hikers say there's nothing that can compare with the feeling of accomplishment they get when they reach the end of the trail without anyone else's help. For the rest of their lives, they enjoy the memories of what they saw and did on their trip. They know that they didn't give up when they faced a challenge. ◆

---

**QUESTIONS**

1. Where does the Appalachian National Scenic Trail begin and end?
2. Which of the trails is the longest? Which is the least difficult?
3. What makes the CDT the most rugged trail?
4. Why would you dissolve iodine tablets in pond water?
5. Would you like to try a long-distance hike on one of these trails someday? Why or why not?

Of the 8,000 museums in the United States, only the Cockroach Hall of Fame displays Liberoachi and a roach's dream vacation.

# CURIOUS COLLECTIONS

*Are there museums for everything?*

1  You walk into a room and see a dead cockroach dressed in a white mink cape seated at the keyboard of a tiny piano. Another dead cockroach is lounging in a small beach chair with tiny sandals by its side. Someone offers you a barbecue-flavored insect larva.[1] Are you trapped in the middle of a strange nightmare? No, you are walking through the Cockroach Hall of Fame. There really is such a place, and it is in Plano, Texas. The Cockroach Hall of Fame is one of many strange and unusual museums you can visit in this country.

2  There are more than 8,000 museums in the United States. Some are huge, with long corridors and high ceilings; others are small, perhaps only one room in a private home. Some large art,

---

[1] larva: the immature, wormlike form of many insects; the larva undergoes changes to develop into the mature form of the insect.

history, and science museums—such as the Smithsonian Institution's Air and Space Museum—are famous. Others, such as the Cockroach Hall of Fame, are unknown to most of us. This article will introduce you to five offbeat[2] institutions that are unknown to most people.

### Kansas Barbed Wire Museum

3 Imagine the fun of seeing more than 1,000 kinds of barbed wire at the Kansas Barbed Wire Museum in LaCrosse, Kansas. Get ready for the Barbed Wire Hall of Fame and for the dioramas showing the many uses of barbed wire throughout history. On display is a raven's nest built mostly of barbed wire. The nest was found in a tree in Kansas during the 1960s. Many types of barbed wire at the museum came from private collections. One collector, for example, had been squirreling away samples of barbed wire for more than 25 years.

**One tough bird made this nest of barbed wire.**

_____

[2] offbeat: unusual; out of the ordinary

### Bananas, Anyone?

4   This museum, too, began as a private collection. About 20 years ago, the founder of the Banana Museum in Auburn, Washington, bought a T-shirt in Hawaii on which the word *banana* was misspelled. This chance happening started her on the road to becoming a banana collector. She now has more than 3,600 banana items in her house, including banana art, books, magnets, cookie jars, toothbrushes, and even banana boxer shorts.

**Yes, we have bananas! We're at the Banana Museum in Auburn, Washington.**

While visitors inspect banana clocks and banana phones, they can listen to banana songs, such as "Yes! We Have No Bananas" and "The Banana Boat Song." If you want to visit, look for the house with the banana wreath on the door. You will be asked to sign the guest book—with a banana pen, naturally.

### Around the World with Dirt

5    The Museum of Dirt, in Boston, Massachusetts, houses over 300 samples of dirt. The founder of the museum started collecting dirt, rather than buying souvenirs, when he traveled. People who heard of his hobby started sending him their own dirt samples from around the world, and the museum was born. There are soil samples from every continent. The dirt comes in a variety of colors—brown, red, white, and even blue and pink.

6    Many famous places are represented in this collection. For example, here you can find dirt from the Great Wall of China; from the Alamo[3] in San Antonio, Texas; and from Mount Everest in Tibet. Some dirt samples are from the backyards of famous people. In case you want to send some dirt from your own backyard, you might like to know the founder is accepting samples.

### The Ones That Didn't Get Away

7    Do you know where the world's largest fish is? Here's a hint: It is not in an ocean or a lake. Instead, you can find it at the National Freshwater Fishing Hall of Fame in Hayward, Wisconsin. The highlight of this museum is a gigantic muskie, a type of freshwater fish. This

--------

[3] Alamo: a fort in Texas where a famous battle was fought in 1836

**It looks like this giant muskie has scooped up a mouthful of tourists visiting the National Freshwater Fishing Hall of Fame in Hayward, Wisconsin.**

particular muskie is four-and-a-half stories high and half a city block long (143 feet). It is made of concrete, steel, and fiberglass.[4] You can actually walk through the fish and climb to the observation deck that is in its toothy, open mouth. From there, you can view the other smaller fiberglass fish on the museum grounds. Remember to bring your camera so you can take home a picture of yourself holding onto a fishing pole with a giant trout at the end of the line. The

---

[4] fiberglass: a form of glass made of fine fibers; it is often combined with fabric or plastic

four buildings of the museum have exhibits of rods, reels, and tackle boxes. The museum attracts about 100,000 visitors each summer.

### A Pretzel-Loving City

8   Philadelphia, Pennsylvania, is known for the Liberty Bell, the 76ers,[5] and its pretzels. At almost every downtown street corner, vendors[6] sell soft pretzels that customers dip in mustard. The number of pretzels that the average Philadelphian eats is 12 times the national average. People there love pretzels so much that they have built a Pretzel Museum. When you visit, be sure to catch the seven-minute movie about the history of the pretzel. Study the assortment of pretzel photos and learn some little-known pretzel trivia. (Did you know that German kids wear pretzels around their necks for good luck on New Year's Day?) You can practice twisting your own pretzels, and before you leave, you can stop at the snack bar that sells (big surprise!) pretzels.

### Other Choices

9   Perhaps reading about these museums has made you curious about other museums. The National Museum of Roller Skating has the world's largest

---

[5] 76ers: Philadelphia's professional basketball team
[6] vendor: a person who sells something

collection of old roller skates. Would you like to learn all sorts of useful facts about the sponge? Head to Spongeorama. You might enjoy the Souvenir Spoons Museum or the Toaster Museum or the Merry-Go-Round Museum. There are plenty of odd museums to visit in this country. Just think of something that interests you, and chances are good that someone has started a museum for it. If no one has opened a museum dedicated to your favorite thing, why don't you start collecting? Maybe someday you can open your own unusual museum. ◆

**QUESTIONS**

1. About how many kinds of barbed wire are on display at the Kansas Barbed Wire Museum?

2. What was the first banana item that the founder of the Banana Museum bought?

3. How did the Museum of Dirt get its start?

4. What are some things you can do at the Pretzel Museum?

5. What makes odd museums such as the ones described in this article enjoyable?

Each year, hurricanes pose a significant danger for people who live along ocean coasts. Computer-generated images of hurricanes, such as this one of Hurricane Fran (1989), can help meteorologists predict a storm's path.

# HURRICANE!

*Why do people on the coasts fear hurricanes?*

1   The news is all over the radio. A hurricane is headed this way. Tourists are told to evacuate as quickly as possible. Store owners plan to board up their windows and close early. Police and fire departments call in extra workers. Homeowners stock up on milk, bread, and drinking water—just in case. What is causing all this commotion? Why are people so afraid of these storms called hurricanes?

2   A quick look at a recent hurricane should explain what all the fuss is about. In 1992 Hurricane Andrew slammed into the southeast coast of the United States. It killed 61 people and caused billions of dollars of damage in Louisiana and Florida. At least 125,000 homes were damaged, leaving about 300,000 people homeless. Almost 10 percent of Florida's farmland was ruined. Power lines were

**Wind lashes trees and drives the sea over barriers as a hurricane attacks Miami, Florida.**

destroyed, leaving about 1 million people without electricity. The damage was so widespread that even a week after the storm, some people were still without power. All this damage was caused by a hurricane. If one were coming your way, wouldn't you be concerned?

### The Birth of a Hurricane

3 Hurricanes are born near the equator in warm ocean waters, usually in the late summer or early fall. Seawater warmed by the sun evaporates and forms huge storm clouds. As the warm air rises,

cooler air rushes in to take its place. A strong wind starts spinning and spiraling[1] upward. At first the wind blows slowly. As more and more air rushes in, the wind grows stronger. Once the wind speed reaches 74 miles per hour (mph), the storm is called a hurricane.

4    The hurricane's winds rotate at a high speed around a calm center called the eye. If you were in the eye, you would see a cloudless sky above you and feel only a light breeze. It is so calm there that many people have mistaken the eye for the end of the storm. They have come out of their shelters, only to be struck by winds coming from the other side of the hurricane.

### The Power of a Hurricane

5    Hurricanes don't stand still. Instead, winds drive them across the sea at speeds of up to 30 mph. Most hurricanes remain at sea and are harmless, but others veer off toward land. When a

---

[1] spiraling: winding; circling around a central point

hurricane hits land, it brings high winds and heavy rains. It can kill people and destroy property in four ways.

6 • Winds: Severe winds of up to 200 mph can pick up cars and boats or uproot trees. They can tear off roofs or knock down entire buildings. In fact, few buildings in the path of a hurricane come through undamaged.

7 • Rain: Heavy rainfall floods basements and streets. Flooding makes travel treacherous[2] or impossible.

8 • Tornadoes: Hurricanes often produce tornadoes, which are spinning columns of air. Winds inside some tornadoes are incredibly powerful. Fortunately, most tornadoes last less than 10 minutes.

9 • Storm surge: Beneath the eye of the hurricane, a wall of water builds up. This water is sucked upward by the low air pressure in the eye of the hurricane. The wall of water is called a storm surge. It may reach heights of 40 feet. When the storm surge hits land, the coast floods immediately, and animals, people, and even buildings can be swept away. Storm surges are responsible for over 90 percent of all hurricane deaths.

---

[2] treacherous: dangerous

## Hurricane Trivia

10 These fierce storms are known by different
names in different parts of the world. In the
Atlantic Ocean and the Caribbean Sea,[3] they are
called *hurricanes*. In the Pacific Ocean, they are
called *typhoons*. In the Indian Ocean and near
Australia, they are called *tropical cyclones*.
Hurricanes behave differently in different parts of
the world. In the Southern Hemisphere, hurricane
winds rotate clockwise. In the Northern
Hemisphere they rotate counter-clockwise.

**Wind speeds around the eye of a hurricane can reach well
over 100 miles an hour.**

[3] Caribbean Sea: a sea bounded by the West Indies,
Central America, and South America

11    Weather forecasters give names to hurricanes to make them easier to track. The first hurricane of the year is given a name starting with *A,* the second with *B,* and so on through the alphabet. At one time all the names were female, but now the names alternate[4] between male and female.

### Predicting Hurricanes

12    Weather experts in many parts of the world keep track of storms that may develop into hurricanes. Weather satellites send pictures of cloud patterns back to Earth. Thousands of weather stations around the world feed data into computers and make the data available to experts. Weather planes and balloons gather more information.

13    Perhaps the most dangerous way to investigate storms is by hurricane hunting. Pilots known as hurricane hunters fly their planes directly into the eye of a hurricane. As they travel, they measure air pressure and wind speed and then send their findings back to forecasters at the National Hurricane Center in Miami. Experts there use the data to predict whether the storm is growing or fading and to guess where the storm might head next. Then they can decide what kind of warning to issue to people in the hurricane's path.

---

[4] alternate: take turns

**Dazed survivors stand in the wreckage of their neighborhood in Galveston, Texas, after a hurricane and storm surge destroyed much of the city in 1900.**

### This Is a Warning!

14   The lowest level of official warning is a Hurricane Watch. A watch tells people in a specific area that there is a 50 percent chance that a hurricane will strike within the next 36 hours. It warns people to keep checking the latest weather news. It also gives residents a chance to prepare their property for a storm. The next level up is a Hurricane Warning. A Hurricane Warning means that a hurricane is likely to strike soon. It announces that an area is in immediate danger and that people should take action quickly to protect themselves and their property.

15      Years ago there was no system of hurricane warnings. In 1900 the deadliest hurricane in United States history hit Galveston, Texas. At that time, Galveston was a growing town. The town's highest point was less than 10 feet above sea level. When the hurricane struck in September 1900, a storm surge 20 feet high flooded the town. Six thousand people, more than one-seventh of the population of Galveston, died. Ten thousand people were left homeless, and half the town was destroyed.

**Today and the Future**

16   Today's methods of hurricane prediction would prevent this horrible loss of life. People would be warned to get out of the storm's path. Still, we don't know enough about hurricanes to feel confident about our safety. Weather experts are still unsure why some storms become hurricanes and others do not. Another mystery is why some hurricanes stay at sea, whereas others strike land. Even with modern methods, experts cannot predict exactly what path a hurricane will take. Hurricanes often swerve unexpectedly, so predictions may be as much as 100 miles off target.

17      Weather experts are trying not only to solve today's problems but also to look to the future. Many scientists think that the earth is going through a global warming. That is, they

believe that temperatures all over the earth are rising. Because hurricanes start in warm ocean water, many experts think that global warming will cause more hurricanes and stronger hurricanes in the future.

18 Every day scientists are learning more about these violent, destructive storms. There is still a great deal more to learn, however. We know we will never be able to control nature. But someday we should be better equipped to protect ourselves from the dangers of hurricanes. ◆

---

**QUESTIONS**
1. What is the eye of a hurricane?
2. What are hurricanes in the Pacific Ocean called?
3. How are hurricanes assigned their names?
4. Name two ways weather forecasters get information about hurricanes.
5. What are residents supposed to do when they receive a Hurricane Warning?
6. Where and when did the most deadly United States hurricane hit?

In Shaker communities, men and women lived and worked separately as brothers and sisters.

# THE SHAKERS

## Living the Simple Life

*Who made the simple, beautiful Shaker furniture that is so popular today?*

1   Oval wooden boxes, such as those below are called Shaker boxes. They are named for the people who made them years ago. The group we call Shakers also made beautiful, simple furniture that is popular with collectors all over the world. In the 1850s, there were several thousand Shakers in America, but only a handful of Shakers are alive today. What happened to the Shakers? What do we know about Shakers and their gift for making beautiful objects?

Dance was a major part of Shaker worship services. This picture shows an organized dance, but wilder, dance-like movements of earlier Shakers gave the group their name.

## Mother Ann and the Beginning of the Shakers

2 The history of the Shakers begins with a woman named Ann Lee, who was born in England about 1736. Ann believed that God spoke through her in a special way. Ann shared her ideas with others and attracted a small group of followers. The group formed a new religion. In 1774 they sailed to America, hoping to find a place to practice their new religion in peace.

3 The group named itself the United Society of Believers in Christ's Second Appearing. But the believers were usually called Shakers because of the unusual way they worshiped. As part of their services, they would tremble, shake, twirl, and dance. Some people said they were trying to shake away their sins.

## Shaker Beliefs

4 Shakers were not always welcome in America, mostly because their beliefs were strange to most people of the time. Here are some of those beliefs:

5 • Men and women are equal. From the beginning, Shaker women held positions of responsibility in the community.

6 • The best life is a simple life, on a farm, far away from the world's temptations. Shakers bought land and set up their own villages away from towns and cities.

7 • Everyone deserves love and care, not just family members. Shakers wanted to prevent members from becoming overly attached to their own relatives and forgetful of the needs of others. Husbands, wives, and children were separated from each other when families joined the Shakers.

8 • People should not be attached to money and power. Individual Shakers owned nothing; all property belonged to the whole community.

9 • All wars are evil. Shakers refused to fight in wars.

### The Shaker Way of Life

10   Shakers' beliefs affected every part of their lives. They lived simply and quietly. For example, they tried not to attract attention with their clothes. Women wore dark-colored dresses with blue and white aprons and close-fitting white bonnets. Men were clean-shaven. Their hair was cut straight across in the front and grew long in the back.

11   Shakers lived in large homes in "families" of 30 to 100 members. Members, called sisters and brothers, shared all the duties of their families. Every sister would take a turn at jobs such as sewing, cooking, laundering, and gardening. Every brother would take a turn at jobs such as gardening, blacksmithing, carpentry, or caring for the animals on their farms.

12   Shakers had rules for even the smallest of actions. For example, there were rules that said that the right foot must be placed on the step first when a member climbed the stairs. When folding hands, the right thumb must cover the left thumb. At meal times, Shakers always sat in groups of four with one platter of food placed between them. All four ate from the same plate, but each person had his or her own spoon. Men and women were separated at most times. They even came to their worship services through separate doors and used separate stairs.

13   Music was an important part of Shaker life. Shakers believed that some of their members

actually communicated with angels. At times, these lucky members felt inspired to sing new songs that they had heard from the angels. Other Shakers would write down these songs as quickly as possible. They would then use these heavenly songs at their worship services.

**From 60 to 80 sisters and brothers lived here, in the largest home in the Shaker Village of Pleasant Hill, Kentucky.**

**Living a Perfect Life**

14   Shakers constantly aimed at perfection. They tried to make their homes spotless, believing that clean rooms attracted good spirits. Every box, tool, or piece of furniture they made had to be made perfectly and without unnecessary decoration. If the object did what it was meant to do in an efficient way, it was perfect. This belief led Shakers to produce objects that were both useful and beautiful.

15   Shakers eagerly accepted new inventions that could help them do their jobs more efficiently. Shakers themselves are known for many inventions, including the clothespin, a simple washing machine, and the swivel chair. They found ways to make money for their communities by selling seeds, furniture, and livestock.[1] Anyone buying a Shaker product could be sure of its high quality and value.

**The Rise and Fall of the Shakers**

16   Throughout the first half of the 19th century, the Shakers attracted thousands of members. White and African-American men, women, and children were all welcome in the fast-growing group. Just before the Civil War, more than 6,000 Shakers lived in 18 Shaker communities in New England, Ohio, and Kentucky. After the war, for a variety

[1] livestock: animals kept for use on a farm or raised to sell

of reasons, members began drifting away from the simple Shaker way of life. In addition, few new members joined. Shaker beliefs did not allow marriage, so membership could not increase from within the group.

**Shakers hung their chairs on pegs so that they could clean the floors more easily.**

17    Slowly the older members started dying and the communities began to wither away. Shakers opened their doors and hearts to orphans and homeless families, hoping they would become members of the group. But only a few people made a lifelong commitment.[2] Throughout the 1880s and 1890s, most of the remaining Shakers sold their land and moved to the few surviving villages.

18    By the year 2001, all but one of the Shaker communities had closed. The Sabbathday Lake community in Maine was home to only seven Shakers. They carried on the tradition of Shaker living and retold the Shaker story to interested visitors.

-------------------

[2]commitment: a pledge; a promise

### Shaker Arts and Crafts

19   The Shakers' desire for perfection in everything they made gave their arts and crafts a special beauty. One writer, when describing Shaker furniture, said "The peculiar grace of a Shaker chair is due to the fact that it was made by someone capable of believing that an angel might come and sit on it."

20   Today, interest in Shaker furniture is at an all-time high. Simple pieces such as tables and chairs are worth tens of thousands of dollars. Small wooden boxes that were made with care more than 100 years ago sell for hundreds of dollars. Collectors love the simple, uncluttered lines of these objects. They admire the fine workmanship that a sister or brother put into the piece. Collectors will never know the names of the women or men who worked on these objects, because Shakers did not sign their work. However, the spirit with which the items were made can still be seen today.

## Visiting a Shaker Village

21 Anyone who would like to glimpse the Shaker way of life can visit one of the Shaker museums in New England, Ohio, or Kentucky. Perhaps you will have a chance to stay overnight in an old Shaker home at Pleasant Hill, Kentucky. If you listen hard, you may be able to hear the peaceful voices of the Shakers singing this hymn:

*'Tis a gift to be simple, 'tis a gift to be free,*

*'Tis a gift to come down where we ought to be,*

*And when we find ourselves in the place just right,*

*We'll be in the valley of love and delight.* ◆

---

**QUESTIONS**

1. Why did Ann Lee come to America?
2. Why were Ann Lee's followers called Shakers?
3. How many people belonged to the Shaker communities at the peak of membership?
4. Why have almost all the Shaker villages closed?
5. Why do collectors like Shaker objects and furniture?

It's never too early to start work on your first million. Here, students in an investors' club study the financial pages of a newspaper. Some teenagers have already been successful in the business world.

# TEEN TITANS OF BUSINESS

*How did three teenagers make their marks on the business world?*

1    Most people would like to be millionaires, but few of us expect that wish to come true. Here are profiles of three young people who were well on their way to their first million by the time they hit their teen years. At four years of age, Mary Rodas became a consultant[1] in an area that was a natural for a kid—toys. David Leung entered the stock market at the ripe old age of ten. And Farrah Gray was an entrepreneur[2] [ŏn´trə prə nûr´] at eight.

---

[1] consultant: an expert who is called on for professional or technical opinions or advice

[2] entrepreneur: a person who organizes and manages a business

### Mary Rodas

2    Mary's father, an immigrant from El Salvador, was the superintendent of an apartment building in New Jersey. One day he let his four-year-old daughter tag along when he visited a tenant, Donald Spector, a toy developer. Spector was laying floor tiles, and Mary pointed out some mistakes he had made. Instead of being put off by her brash[3] attitude, Spector thought that Mary might be able to evaluate toys as well. When he invited Mary to play with some toys he was working on, the little girl had plenty to say about them. Spector soon discovered that Mary was worth listening to. For several years, he brought her toys to test, and in time Spector hired her. At 14, when she helped develop and launch a new toy called Balzac, Mary was named vice president of marketing at Catco, Spector's toy company.

3    Mary loved the work despite the difficulties. "Becoming a VP at that age is really cool and really neat," she said later. "The only difference is that I needed to make my own way and break through the barriers because a lot of people didn't take me seriously at first. They thought it was a hoax."[4]

4    Balzac, a brightly colored balloon ball available with various objects inside, proved that

---

[3] brash: bold; rude
[4] hoax: a trick; an act meant to deceive

her appointment was not a hoax. In seven years, under Mary's supervision, this simple ball inspired 30 other toys. Meanwhile, Mary completed high school at a school for professional children—mostly actors, musicians, and dancers with erratic[5] schedules. Too young to get a driver's license, she was driven from

**Largely because of the success of the Balzac toy, Mary Rodas became president of Catalyst Toys.**

school to her office in a limo. Then she went on to New York University to study communications—but only part-time. At 23 she became the youngest president of a toy company when she was named president of Catalyst Toys, another company owned by Donald Spector.

5   In an interview when she was 21, Mary had these words of advice: "Always grab the opportunities as they come and always be happy.

---

[5] erratic: irregular; not predictable

Life is short. Just go with it. . . . You never know what's going to happen the next day . . . so if you really want to succeed, go after it."

**David Leung**

6   David Leung's parents wanted to encourage him to save for college. So when he was 10 years old, they rewarded his good grades and success in math contests with a gift of stocks. The catch was that he had to choose the stocks that they would buy in his name. After studying the stock market and thinking about his own experience with computers, David selected a software company for his first purchase. Then he was hooked on the stock market. Almost all the money he received as gifts or made from installing and repairing computers went into stocks.

7       David began buying at a good time, when the market was going up, and he made good choices. Within a few years, his stocks were worth about $550,000! Then the market hit rough times, and David's high-tech[6] stocks slipped. At 17 he had a mere $450,000 in stocks, give or take $20,000.

8       David doesn't believe he has a special gift for stock picking. Instead, he credits his success to saving cash and studying the market. These are things anyone can do, he says. "It doesn't matter

---

[6] high-tech: scientific technology that involves highly advanced electronic systems or devices

**David Leung began his investing career at age 10. Now he advises other teens.**

how much you save, as long as you get in the habit."

9    David's approach to investing is to research the companies that interest him and to invest in what he knows. He sticks with a stock for years, not letting the daily ups and downs of the market get to him. In his first seven years of investing, he traded only 20 times. Trying to guess which way the market will go, he believes, is about the same as gambling.

10    At 13, to help other teens understand how they can get into stocks, David founded his first Web site, Investing for Kids. Four years later, with the help of other students and teachers in his California high school, he started another site, Invest Smart. It offers not only advice but also a real-time investment game, now used in more than 9,000 schools nationwide. In this game, you are given $100,000 of imaginary money to buy

and sell stocks and mutual funds. The program tracks the value of your picks so you can see how well your investments pay off. David's sites receive well over 1 million hits daily.

11    David entered the Massachusetts Institute of Technology in the fall of 2000. Perhaps by the time he graduates, he will be starting work on his second million.

## Farrah Gray

12    When Farrah Gray was 6 years old, his 22-year-old brother, Andre, began making business trips to Europe and Asia. Andre offered to take Farrah along to his business meetings. Farrah recalls, "I remember thinking it would be a good adventure. I was just listening and being a sponge. I think that's where the seeds were planted"—the seeds for an early and remarkable career in business. After Farrah returned home from his travels, he had business cards printed, calling himself a "21st Century CEO."[7]

13    At eight years of age, Farrah formed his first company, the Urban Neighborhood Economic Enterprise Club (UNEEC). He and 14 other Chicago kids between the ages of 8 and 13 thought up a dozen or more moneymaking projects. Then they contacted parents, teachers,

---

[7] CEO: chief executive office; the person in charge of day-to-day operations of a company

politicians, and local businesspeople for start-up money. They raised $15,000, kept some in reserve, and put the rest into various projects—for example, a lemonade stand, a cookie-baking-and-selling endeavor, and an Internet comic book. Five of the projects made money, enough to pay a little back to the investors as well as $20 to splurge on video games. The

**At the age of six, Farrah Gray decided to become a "21st Century CEO." He has already succeeded.**

rest of the profits went back into the reserve fund to support the next moneymaking idea. By the time Farrah was 16, the fund had grown to $300,000, and Farrah had set up a Web site to invite entrepreneurs to apply for start-up funds. His company, now named New Early Entrepreneur Wonders, or NE2W, limits its investments to companies headed by people under 23 years of age.

14    However, one company was not enough to keep Farrah busy. Before he was 16 years old, he had started these companies as well:

- Farr-Out Foods, which develops foods targeted at kids and teens; its first product was Farr-Out Strawberry-Vanilla Pancake Syrup.
- a company that helps entrepreneurs looking for start-up money; the entrepreneurs are matched with a database[8] of more than 100,000 possible investors and lenders.
- a production company that sponsors and produces public service programming for teens; the company operates in Las Vegas, where Farrah now lives.
- Farrah Gray Enterprises, which handles Farrah's speaking engagements. He is a popular speaker who receives fees of from $1,000 to $10,000 per appearance.

15    In addition, Farrah has founded his own charitable foundation and serves on the board of directors of the Las Vegas United Way and the board of advisors for the Las Vegas Chamber of Commerce.

16    In 2001, at the age of 16, Farrah was the keynote speaker at the annual community recognition luncheon of the California Black

---

[8] database: a large collection of data, contained on a computer, that has been organized in such a way that the pieces of the information can easily be used

Chamber of Commerce. Despite the many speeches and TV interviews he has given since he was 11 years old, he admitted, "I had a million butterflies before I spoke."

17    Farrah insists that he was an ordinary teenager with extraordinary goals. And his advice to others? "If you don't have a goal, make it your goal to get a goal." ◆

---

**QUESTIONS**

1. How did Mary Rodas get into the business of toymaking?
2. How has David Leung tried to help other teens achieve financial success?
3. What was Farrah Gray's first business?
4. How has Farrah tried to help the community?
5. The article includes advice from each of the three entrepreneurs. Whose advice are you most likely to follow? Why?

# Strange Stories

## of the

## *Sea*

*When is a fish tale more than a myth?*

1 True or false?
- Sea monsters have been lurking deep underwater for hundreds of years.
- An entire continent called Atlantis sank under the ocean.
- Mermaids are sea creatures who are part human and part fish.

Is there truth to any of these statements? Your first reaction might be a strong NO. But don't be so sure. We don't know everything about what's in the seas.

### There's Something About Coelacanths

2 When most people think of sea monsters hiding underwater, Nessie comes to mind. Nessie is the mysterious creature that has often been sighted in

During the Middle Ages, sailors feared attacks by gigantic sea monsters. Perhaps not all legends about the sea are entirely fantasies. Some of them may have a basis in fact.

57

Loch Ness, a large lake in Scotland. Some people have even taken photos of the Loch Ness monster, but the pictures are so unclear that people do not agree on what they show. Considering that Loch Ness is completely surrounded by land, most people believe that a real monster would have been caught or identified long ago. There is a great deal of doubt that a sea monster actually lives in Loch Ness.

3     Sea monsters in the open ocean, however, are another topic altogether. Do you agree that this qualifies as a monster: a six-foot fish, with a hinged skull and thick scales that are lined with toothpick-like points, that has been around for 410 million years?

4     For many years, the coelacanth [sē´lə kănth] was thought to be extinct. Fossils[1] of ancient coelacanths were found on every continent except Antarctica. This fish, usually about 18 inches long, could be identified by its unusual tail. The tail was divided into three parts, and an extra trunk and fin jutted out from the middle of the tail. The head, too, was remarkable. The tiny brain was squeezed into a small part of the skull so that the rest of the skull could open with the mouth. That allowed the fish to swallow much larger portions of food than the mouth alone could take in.

---

[1] fossil: the hardened remains or imprints of a plant or animal that lived in previous ages

**The coelacanth, once thought to be extinct, has not changed in 410 million years.**

Scientists believed that the coelacanth, which first appeared twice as long ago as dinosaurs did, died out 65 million years ago.

5    In 1938, however, a museum curator[2] in South Africa visited the fishing boat of a friend. In a pile of fish, rays, and sharks, she saw a blue fish with an unusual tail. She asked for the fish, and somehow got a cab driver to carry her and the five-foot long dead fish back to the museum. There she contacted a local expert on fish, who identified the blue fish as a coelacanth.

6    Another coelacanth was found in the same area of the Indian Ocean in 1952. More coelacanths have been found near Madagascar,

---

[2] curator: a person in charge of a museum or similar institution

near Indonesia, and South Africa. No one can explain how this fish has persisted, with almost no changes, for more than 400 million years.

## Going Out with a Bang

7 The story of the lost continent of Atlantis was written in Greece as early as 300 B.C. According to the story, the people of Atlantis were successful but very proud and greedy. As a punishment from the gods, the continent was shaken by explosions and plunged to the bottom of the Atlantic Ocean. In the 2,000 years since the story was written, many people have searched for this sunken land. However, none of its rich ruins have ever been found.

8 Many scientists today believe that the searchers were looking in the wrong body of water. They think that the story of Atlantis was based on what happened to the island of Santorini, Greece, in the Aegean Sea.

9 Around 2000 B.C., when Santorini was called Thira, the people of the island were part of the Minoan [mĭ nō´ ən] civilization. Very successful traders, they were rich and advanced for their time. Then, around 1600 B.C., the volcano on Thira erupted. The volcano spewed out seven cubic miles[3] of melted rock. Parts of the island

---

[3] cubic mile: an area 1 mile wide, 1 mile long, and 1 mile high

were blown away. In the earthquakes that followed, other parts sank under the water. The parts that were left were blanketed by ash. The eruption on Thira caused tidal waves that flooded nearby islands, carrying away people and property. The destruction was so great that the entire Minoan civilization came to an end.

10    In recent years, researchers have compared Greek and Egyptian accounts of the disaster and discovered clues to where "Atlantis" was. They have dug under the mountains of ash on Santorini and discovered long-buried streets, homes, and businesses. Are these the streets of Atlantis? No one knows for sure.

### The *Little* Mermaid?

11    Mermaids appear in folklore[4] in both Europe and Africa. They are creatures who are women from head to waist and fish from the waist down. According to some stories, mermaids could place human men in

Images and descriptions of mermaids appeared as early as the eighth century B.C.

[4] folklore: the unwritten stories, myths, and legends of a culture

**Compare this West Indian manatee with the mermaid pictured on page 61. Are there any similarities?**

a trance and magically take them to live underwater. Is it possible that the beautiful mermaids were based on a relative of the elephant?

12    The manatee [măn´ə tē] is a mammal that lives in warm water, spending most of its time eating water plants. The largest of the various kinds of manatees can grow as long as 13 feet and weigh more than 2,000 pounds. The manatee has front legs shaped like paddles and no hind legs. Its large body ends in a rounded fin instead of a tail. This gentle and playful animal moves rather slowly but gracefully through water. Manatees have been seen playing follow-the-leader and bodysurfing. Because the manatee is a mammal

rather than a fish, it must poke its head above water for air every three or four minutes. Manatees are active mostly at night.

13    Modern researchers believe that long ago sailors saw gray manatees rising out of dark water at night and thought they were looking at women. Then, when the sailors saw the manatees' rear fins, the idea of the mermaid was born.

14    Nobody can explain how a fish that swam in oceans 400 million years ago is still around. Nobody can prove absolutely that Thira is the real Atlantis or that manatees are the real mermaids. What do you think?

---

## QUESTIONS

1. Why do many people doubt the existence of the Loch Ness monster?
2. How were coelacanth fossils identified?
3. Why are living coelacanths so remarkable?
4. What caused much of the island of Santorini to sink below the Aegean Sea?
5. Do you agree with the theory that mermaids are based on manatees? Why or why not?

# Learning About You

*How can you learn more about that fascinating topic—yourself?*

1   What could be more interesting to you than you? For thousands of years, people have been studying their own personalities. They have examined their likes, dislikes, interests, strengths, and weaknesses. We would all like to understand ourselves better so we can choose careers and lifestyles that make us happy. Over time, people have discovered many ways to learn about themselves.

## What Is Personality?

2   Personality is the pattern of behaving, thinking, and feeling that makes each person unique. A personality is made up of two parts. One part consists of the traits[1] that we inherit from our

---

[1] trait: a quality or characteristic of a person

**Do you like to take risks, like this mountain climber? Or is your idea of fun sitting by a warm fire with a good book? Knowing your own personality type helps you choose the activities that will give you the most pleasure.**

parents. The other part develops as we react to our environment and to the people and events around us. It's hard to tell which parts of a personality come from genes[2] and which are shaped by one's environment.

3    Within a few years after birth, a person's unique personality is set. Though we all have new experiences as we get older, our personalities change very little. Our basic interests, likes, dislikes, skills, and habits remain remarkably stable throughout our lives.

### Are There Reliable Ways to Reveal Personality?

4  For centuries people believed in astrology [ə sträl´ə jē]. Astrologists believe that personalities are determined by the location of the sun, the moon, and the planets at the exact moment a person is born. They think that these heavenly bodies can control the way people feel, the way they approach problems, and the way they work with others.

5    By the 19th century, few people really believed that stars and planets had much effect on personality. Some people began to look for answers about personality in a completely different way. In the 1890s, phrenologists [frə näl´ə jĭsts]

---

[2] gene: a tiny unit that carries the qualities, such as hair or eye color, that parents pass on to their children

believed that they could learn all about personality from the shape of a person's skull and the bumps on his or her head. They believed that a person with a bump in a certain part of the skull would be creative. A bump in a different part of the skull meant a person was cautious. Today, few people take this so-called science seriously.

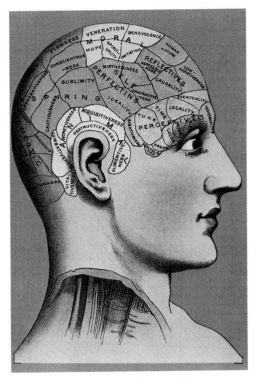

**Phrenologists mapped areas of the head that were thought to control personality traits.**

6    Can you learn much about a person's personality by studying his or her handwriting? Handwriting analysts believe you can. They feel that the pressure, shape, slant, and spacing of a person's writing reveal a great deal about personality. For example, according to handwriting analysis, people who press down hard on their pencils are pushy. Those who don't press down hard suffer from poor health. People who write using rounded letters are warmhearted. Those who write using pointed

letters are good at organizing. Most scientists, however, do not consider handwriting analysis to be a serious, reliable way to understand personality.

### Why Test Personality?

7 Psychologists [sī kӓl´ ə jĭsts], scientists who study the way the mind works, have developed personality tests that are more reliable than astrology or handwriting analysis. People who take these tests do so for a variety of reasons. One reason is to understand themselves better. From the results of personality tests, people may learn a great deal about how they approach life and how they deal with problems. They may see how they usually handle their feelings, how they view other people, and how other people see them.

8 Another reason to test personality is to reveal a person's interests and skills. Such a test may help someone to identify the perfect career or at least to avoid a career that he or she is not suited for. For example, a personality test might reveal that you are a very patient person. In that case, you might choose a career that requires patience, such as teaching students with learning problems or doing scientific research. Suppose you found out that you do your best work when you are by yourself. If so, you probably wouldn't choose to work as a salesperson, who must interact with others all day.

9    Sometimes personality tests are used to decide who should work together on a project. Suppose you are setting up a project that requires many workers. It would probably be a mistake to assign to the team only people who had the personality traits of leaders. They might have difficulty deciding who was in charge. Studying the results of personality tests could help you choose team members who have compatible[3] traits.

**Groups often work most effectively when they include members with different personality types.**

_____

[3] compatible: able to work well together

### A Modern Personality Test

10    To identify individuals' personalities, psychologists
today usually give written or spoken tests. One
popular personality test is the Myers-Briggs Type
Inventory. This test was first given in the 1960s.
The test asks hundreds of multiple-choice
questions like the following:

☞ *At parties, do you like to*
*a) stay late     b) leave early*

☞ *When you do a job, are you likely to*
*a) do it the same way every time*
*b) try to find a new way to do the job*

11        People with similar personality traits answer
the questions in similar ways. Therefore, a
specialist can study a person's responses to the
questions and identify various aspects[4] of the
person's personality. The process helps people
learn about their own personalities. Knowing
your personality type can help you appreciate the
positive aspects of your personality and
emphasize your strengths.

---

[4] aspect: any of the possible ways in which something can
be considered

### A Warning About Pop-Psych

12   Personality tests can be useful when people with special training give them and explain them. However, many of the tests you find in magazines or on the Internet are meant to be taken just for fun. A lot of the information in these sources is popular psychology, or pop-psych. Pop-psych uses language that sounds like real psychology, but it offers simple answers to complex questions. If you decide to take one of these tests, don't believe everything it tells you.

13      Even if you take a serious personality test, you can't expect the test to change your life. All it can do is shed a little light on what your personality is like. What you do with that knowledge is up to you. ◆

---

**QUESTIONS**

1. What is personality?
2. What are the two parts of a personality?
3. What do phrenologists claim reveals a person's personality?
4. Name three reasons that people take personality tests.
5. How reliable are the results of a short personality test you find in a magazine article or on the Internet?

# KALEIDOSCOPES

*How can two mirrors, a cardboard tube, and some tape make the world beautiful?*

1 Have you ever played with a kaleidoscope [kə lī´ də skōp]? Do you remember seeing one sparkling design morph[1] into the next . . . and into another design after that? A kaleidoscope makes a great toy. But "scopes" are not just for children. Adults, too, enjoy seeing the dazzling, jewel-like designs that kaleidoscopes make. Some artists are even inspired by kaleidoscopes! That's fitting, for the word *kaleidoscope* means "to see a beautiful form." A simple kaleidoscope is not difficult to make. Maybe you'd like to try making your own scope and using it to see the world in a new way.

---

[1] morph: to transform from one shape to another

## What Is a Kaleidoscope?

2   To understand how a kaleidoscope works, you need to start with a flat mirror. Imagine looking into that mirror. You see yourself, of course. But the you in the mirror is not identical to the real you. For example, you may wear a watch on your left wrist. But if you were the image looking out of the mirror, that watch would be on your right wrist. The mirror reverses you, left to right.

3     Now imagine looking at a large mirror with three parts, as in a clothing store. In some of these mirrors, the middle part does not move, while the side mirrors can swing toward the middle like doors. If the three parts are in a straight line, you simply see three reflections of yourself. Imagine swinging the side mirrors toward the middle one. Now the mirrors will reflect each other as well as you. Suddenly there are six, seven, eight, or more of you. And each time a mirror reflects an image, it reverses that image. So some of the "yous" that you see are the opposites of the others. The kaleidoscope is based on that effect.

## Putting Together a Kaleidoscope

4   In its simplest form, a kaleidoscope is made up of two flat mirrors an inch or so wide and several inches long. The mirrors are placed next to each other to form a V. When a person brings the angle of the V up to one eye and points the

**Here are the basic parts of a scope: a tube, two mirrors forming a V, a lens, and tiny objects for the object case.**

scope at an object, he or she will see at least three versions of the object: the original and two reflections. All the images spread like points of a star from the point where the mirrors meet.

5    You can make a partial open-ended kaleidoscope by simply holding two flat mirrors together to form a V and bringing them up to your eye. To give the V a permanent shape, join the two mirrors with tape, adding a third side— with a dark surface—between the mirrors. Then place the three-sided object inside a tube. If you want a more finished look to your scope, build it from a kit. Scope kits are available online as well as from some stores. Kits include a clear round glass lens to cover each end of the tube.

6    In most kaleidoscopes, another element[2] is added at one end. A container called the *object case* or *object cell* holds one or more items for viewing. These items may include bits of glass, gemstones, feathers, seashells, or plastic beads filled with colored

**Here is what the U.S. flag looks like as seen through a kaleidoscope.**

liquids. Light enters the object case from the back or side. A viewer looks through the end opposite the object case and turns the kaleidoscope. With each turn, the items shift about in the case, changing the pattern.

7    When you look into a kaleidoscope with two mirrors, you see a star-like pattern. The number of points in the star depends on the angle between the two mirrors.

8    Some kaleidoscopes have more than two mirrors, and the mirrors can be arranged in various ways. When you look into these kaleidoscopes, you may see many identical stars,

---

[2] element: a main part

or a repeated square pattern, or even a 3-D[3] image! What you see depends on the arrangement of the mirrors.

## Today's Kaleidoscopes

9 The kaleidoscope has been popular ever since it was introduced to the public in 1817. Before the invention of radio and television, a large kaleidoscope in the parlor provided family entertainment. Small kaleidoscopes have long been children's toys.

10 During the last 30 years, the kaleidoscope has enjoyed a new burst of development. Artists have created more complex and unusual scopes than ever before. For example, one scope uses soap bubbles as the object. Another uses an entire fishtank as the object case, with the swimming fish creating the pattern. Other scopes project their patterns onto screens for many people to view at once. The largest kaleidoscope in the world is a 60-foot silo[4] in Mount Tremper, New York. There patterns are projected onto a sphere[5] with a diameter of 100 feet.

11 Modern kaleidoscope makers have also focused on the look of the scope itself. Instead of

---

[3] 3-D: three-dimensional; having height, width, and depth
[4] silo: a cylinder-shaped tower where wheat, corn, or other grains are stored
[5] sphere: a round shape, such as a globe or ball

a simple wooden tube, the outside casing may be a sculpture of an animal, a miniature plane, a jewel-covered box, or a more futuristic-looking shape. Like other works of art, each of these kaleidoscopes is named and only a few are produced—sometimes only one. While a basic scope might sell for less than five dollars, these creations may command prices in the hundreds or even thousands of dollars.

12    In addition to actual kaleidoscopes, there are virtual kaleidoscopes: computer programs that produce intricate[6] patterns like those from a real kaleidoscope. Mathematicians and other computer programmers produce these works of art. Often they post their creations online.

13    Do you want to see more kaleidoscope images? You can find photos of scopes and scope patterns in books and on Web sites run by kaleidoscope lovers. Some sites even show movies of a scope's changing patterns. You can start with the address http://www.kaleidoscopeheaven.org or do your own search for *kaleidoscope*.

14    You might decide to buy an inexpensive scope locally or online or to visit one of the shops or sites devoted to rare, expensive versions. You could even join the Brewster Society, an

---

[6] intricate: very complicated

international organization for kaleidoscope fans started in 1986. This society holds an annual convention and presents awards for scopes in such categories as "Favorite Kaleidoscope," "Best Image," and the "Oh Wow! Award." ◆

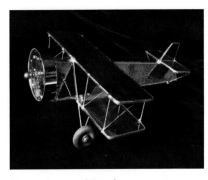

**Even the outside of a scope can be a work of art, such as this airplane kaleidoscope.**

**QUESTIONS**

1. What does the word *kaleidoscope* mean?
2. Explain how a kaleidoscope works, basing your explanation on the example of a three-part mirror.
3. Why do many kaleidoscopes have object cases? What do the object cases do?
4. When was the public first introduced to the kaleidoscope?
5. Describe some of the unusual shapes that modern kaleidoscopes have been made into.

First Ladies have always done more than just stand by their husbands' sides. When the White House was attacked during the War of 1812, Dolley Madison saved such national treasures as the Declaration of Independence.

# The *First First Ladies*

*How did the wives of the early U.S. presidents act in their roles as First Ladies?*

1   Portraits of the wives of the early presidents of the United States usually show elderly ladies who are wearing ruffled bonnets and sitting with their hands folded stiffly on their laps. The real First Ladies were not quite like their paintings. These women had lived through the perils of warfare near their homes, lonely separations from busy husbands, and the challenges of life in a new country. The first woman to serve as First Lady set the standard for all the First Ladies who followed her. The second was an early champion[1] of the rights of women. The third rescued priceless objects in the face of great danger.

---

[1] champion: defender; supporter

**Martha Washington was the
model for later First Ladies.**

### Martha Washington

2   Imagine being the first one ever to do something.
That was what faced Martha Washington as the
wife of the first president of the United States.
The colonies had been ruled by a faraway king.
Now they were a separate nation. What example
should the president and his wife set? Some
people thought they should act like a king and
queen. But Americans had rejected the English
monarchy,[2] so most people wanted the
Washingtons to behave differently.

3   Martha decided to be herself. From her
childhood, she had been taught the skills
necessary to be a gracious and charming hostess.

-----

[2] monarchy: a government headed by a king, queen, or
other ruler who inherits the position

She knew just enough reading, writing, and arithmetic to run a household efficiently. Martha may have been a terrible speller all her life, but she excelled in making people feel at home.

4    For much of their married life, George Washington had been involved in public life. He often was away from his family, first as a delegate[3] to the Continental Congress and later as Commander in Chief of the Continental Army. During those times, the burden of running Mount Vernon, the Washingtons' plantation, fell on Martha's shoulders. So in 1776, when the Revolutionary War began, Martha was ready to do her part. She supervised her servants as they spun cloth for uniforms and bandages, cured more meat than the household could use, and preserved large quantities of fruits and vegetables. When she was not busy with these activities, Martha knitted scarves, stockings, and sweaters for the soldiers.

5    Throughout the war, Martha joined her husband whenever she could. At camp, she found ways to be helpful, such as mending the officers' uniforms. She brought food and clothing to Valley Forge, Pennsylvania, where the troops were stationed one terrible winter. While she was at Valley Forge, Martha was busy from morning

---

[3] delegate: a representative; person given authority to act on behalf of others

**During the terrible winter at Valley Forge, Martha Washington's behind-the-scenes work supported the Commander in Chief and his army.**

until night, organizing nurses and supplies at the temporary hospital, taking food to the needy, and forming groups to aid the wounded soldiers.

6      Later Martha put all her skills to good use as First Lady. Although the presidential home in New York was small and crowded, she was gracious and welcoming toward everyone who visited. She avoided political⁴ discussions and tried to smooth out any disagreements. Martha kept a watchful eye on household expenses and carefully supervised the servants.

---

⁴ political: having to do with the activities and concerns of government

7     When Washington's two terms of office were finished, he and his wife retired to their beloved Mount Vernon. Martha was overjoyed. She wrote to a friend, "I am again fairly settled down to the pleasant duties of an old-fashioned Virginia house-keeper, steady as a clock, busy as a bee, and cheerful as a cricket."

### Abigail Adams

8  As the wife of the vice president, Abigail Adams often assisted Martha Washington at social events. Thus, it was a bit easier for her to assume the role of First Lady when her husband was elected president. Abigail was not the type of person who simply welcomed guests at

**Abigail Adams was an early feminist and a trusted advisor to her husband, John.**

parties. She loved political discussions and enjoyed debating with others.

9     In those days, it was unusual for a woman to express her ideas, especially about politics. But Abigail was an unusual woman. As a child, she appeared serious and quiet. She was smart, but poor health had prevented her from attending school. So Abigail taught herself by reading every book she could find. When she visited her grandparents, she would listen intently as her grandfather and his guests discussed politics.

10    A common interest in politics and books first brought Abigail and John Adams together, and the interest bonded them throughout their marriage. As John became more involved in the movement for independence from England, he often had to leave his family. In his absence, Abigail took care of the children, ran their farm, and managed to write her husband long letters containing information and advice.

11    When John was serving in the Continental Congress, he often shared his wife's letters with other delegates. The letters accurately described the political situation in Massachusetts. Abigail urged her husband to declare that slavery was wrong and to consider giving women the right to vote, own property, and obtain an education.

12    During and after the Revolutionary War, Abigail continued to exchange letters with her husband. They discussed what an independent

country should be like and what rules it should follow. Some of these ideas later became part of the Constitution of the United States.

13    After Adams was elected president, he continued to depend on his wife for advice. They discussed political issues and the work of the government. Abigail would look over John's speeches and make suggestions. In her quiet way, she played a part in the formation of the United States.

### Dolley Madison

14    Dolley Madison brought a completely different spirit to the White House when she became First Lady. She was noted for her love of people and her generous hospitality. The parties she gave were the biggest and fanciest parties that Washington had ever seen, and Dolley was the perfect hostess. Her warm smile and cheerful personality put everyone at ease. She remembered the names of the many guests who came to the White House. She gave equal time and attention to both friends and rivals of her husband. She never gossiped, and she steered conversations away from politics. Her dinners were extravagant, with an abundance of fine foods and drinks.

15    From the time James Madison was named secretary of state for President Thomas Jefferson, Dolley began holding the parties that made her the best-known hostess in the capital. Jefferson, a widower, often called upon the popular Dolley to preside at his White House dinner parties.

16    Dolley was not only a well-loved partygiver, however. She was responsible for saving some national treasures during the War of 1812. In August 1814, enemy British troops marched toward Washington. President Madison was out of the city checking on the federal[5] troops. Dolley was alone in the White House, except for a few servants. Calmly she gathered the original copies of the Constitution and the Declaration of Independence and other valuable papers. She carefully placed them in a small trunk. As she waited for her husband to return, she packed a few other possessions. But the president didn't return to the White House. Instead, a messenger arrived with instructions that Dolley should leave immediately. At the last minute, she took a famous portrait of George Washington with her. With a carriage full of priceless items, Dolley left the city just as the British troops entered from another direction.

17    A few days after the British withdrew, the Madisons returned to Washington. Many buildings had been destroyed by fire. The White House

---

[5] federal: part of the central government of the United States

had been looted and burned. Only the stone walls were standing. The president and First Lady were forced to find another place to live. As the city began the long task of rebuilding, Dolley once again resumed[6] her famous dinner parties.

18    The words *first lady* bring to mind a special group of women who share a distinctive role in the history of the United States. Martha Washington, Abigail Adams, and Dolley Madison were indeed special, as the first of the First Ladies. ◆

---

## QUESTIONS

1. Where did Martha Washington learn the skills that helped her as First Lady?
2. How did Martha Washington help during the Revolutionary War?
3. What ideas did Abigail Adams have about human rights?
4. In what ways did Abigail Adams influence her husband?
5. Why was Dolley Madison such a successful hostess?
6. What items did Dolley Madison save from the British in the War of 1812?

---

[6] resume: to begin again

90

## PHOTO CREDITS

**Cover** Bill Longcore/Photo Researchers; **iii (t)** Courtesy National Freshwater Fishing Hall of Fame, Haywood, WI; **iii (b)** Courtesy Shaker Museum and Library, Old Chatham, NY; **iv** PhotoDisc, Inc.; **vi** John Elk, III/Bruce Coleman, Inc.; **3, 5** Courtesy NPS; **8, 12** PhotoDisc, Inc.; **14** David Young-Wolff/PhotoEdit; **15** Donna Ikenberry/Earth Scenes; **18** Courtesy Coachroach Hall of Fame; **20** Courtesy Kansas Barbed Wire Museum; **21 (t)** Ann Lovell/Washington Banana Museum, Auburn, Washington; **21 (b)** PhotoDisc, Inc.; **23** Courtesy National Freshwater Fishing Hall of Fame, Haywood, WI; **24** PhotoDisc, Inc.; **26** Courtesy NASA; **28–29** Courtesy NOAA; **31** PhotoDisc, Inc.; **33** Courtesy NOAA; **36, 37** Courtesy Shaker Museum and Library, Old Chatham, NY; **38** Scala/Art Resource, NY; **39** Library of Congress; **41, 43** Courtesy Shaker Village of Pleasant Hill, KY; **44** Library of Congress; **46** Stephen Frisch/Stock Boston; **49** Courtesy Mary Rodas; **51** Courtesy David Leung; **53** Jenna Bodnar; **56** Stock Montage; **59** Leonard L.T. Rhodes/Animals Animals; **61** *The Little Mermaid*, E.S. Hardy (19th Century), Private Collection/Bridgeman Art Library, London; **62** Herb Segars/Animals Animals; **64** Maria Nasif/See Jane Run; **67** Bettmann/CORBIS; **69** Tony Freeman/PhotoEdit; **72** Orion Press/Natural Selection; **75** Tony Freeman/PhotoEdit; **76** Adam Peiperl/Corbis Stock Market; **79** Courtesy Linda Bellacicco/Moon Dog Kaleidoscopes; **80** Stock Montage; **82** National Portrait Gallery, Smithsonian Institution/Art Resource, NY; **84** Stock Montage/SuperStock; **85** Bettmann/Corbis; **87** PhotoDisc, Inc.

90